THE
RHYTHM
SECTION

Mark Burnell was born in Northumberland and grew up in Brazil. He is a novelist and screenwriter. His debut novel, *The Rhythm Section*, is the first in a series of thrillers featuring Stephanie Patrick and is now a major motion picture. The film was produced by Eon, the company responsible for the James Bond franchise, and stars Blake Lively and Jude Law. Mark lives in England with his family.

Praise for Mark Burnell:

'If you like thrillers, this is as good as it gets'
Economist

'Utterly gripping – eat your heart out, Jason Bourne'
Observer

'A Casablanca for the 21st century'
Boris Starling, author of *Messiah*

'Mark Burnell brings the espionage novel right up to date'
Sunday Telegraph

Also by Mark Burnell

The Rhythm Section
Chameleon
Gemini
The Third Woman